From Dark to Light

Isabella Murphy

pink umbrella books

PHOENIX, AZ

ISBN: 978-0-9985162-2-6

     Published by Pink Umbrella Books (www.pinkumbrellapublishing.com)

Isabella Murphy- author

 From Dark to Light/ Isabella Murphy.

 The journey of a pumpkin as he goes from small white seed to carved Jack O' Lantern.

ISBN : 978-0-9985162-2-6

 Library of Congress Control Number: 2017952190

Illustrations by Natalia Pérez

Illustrations © 2017 Natalia Pérez

Cover design by Natalia Pérez

Cover portrait by Heidi Alletzhauser

From Dark to Light

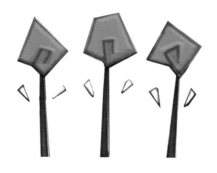

Old Mr. Smith's wife digs a hole
in the moist soil of their farm and gently sets me inside.
As she encloses my space of light and happiness,
fear fills me. A world of darkness surrounds me.
I feel like I'm trapped in a cave. I can't breathe. I wish I could see
the birds flying above.
I want to be free like them.

I started off as a slim, white seed. There is nothing special about me, just a plain, boring, ordinary pumpkin.

I am planted next to my two sisters, Plumpalicious and Plumpilina. We really don't have anything in common. And they don't care about me, since they are girls and I am a boy pumpkin. My name, Pumpker, means "weirdo" in our secret pumpkin language.

Plumpalicious winks at Plumpilina and says, "Snailsnah, blah, blah."

"Creepynah, blah, blah," Plumpilina replies.

"What's that supposed to mean?" I ask. They both giggle and point at me. I don't get their jokes.

I am lonely in the dark cave. The only things in front of me are a dirt wall, a slimy worm, and thick tree roots from above. I move away. The crumbly dirt touches my back, and I know I have nowhere to go.

I don't know how much time passes—every day is the same. But one day I wake up and notice something different. Light pours into my eyes.

As I squint through the brightness, I see green tendrils sprouting from my arms. And when I look over to my right, I can see the faces of my two sisters, who are also rising from the darkness. Their eyes sparkle with awe as they look at the world around them.

More time passes as I continue to grow. Plumpalicious and Plumpilina ignore me even more as they giggle and show off their new, curly tendrils to each other. I'm getting a little bored. This is what I've been wishing for, for such a long time, to be out in the sunlight. But now I want something different. Something wonderful.

I want to be loved by a family.

This Halloween, I will be picked by a boy or girl to bring laughter in some sort of way. I don't know what I will encounter, but I hope it will bring me to tears of joy.

I just can't wait to be picked by a child, and I see that my sisters are anxious too. For once, they forget about their tendrils and focus instead on the excitement that fills the air. We giggle and laugh about it together. This is so nice, having someone to talk to.

I am close to being a full-grown pumpkin now. Just a few more inches to go.

My life so far has been full of changes. Every day is passing by so quickly. I look up and see trees decorated with many colorful leaves. One leaf falls and hits the ground softly. Halloween is coming! I wonder what it will be like at the family's house.

Tomorrow! Tomorrow! I can't stop thinking about that beautiful day when I see the delighted faces of all the children. They'll roam around the pumpkin patch, dragging their parents, pointing out this pumpkin or that.

I went to sleep late last night. I couldn't help thinking about the pumpkin patch. I see cars driving in the parking lot as I slowly wake up.

More and more cars approach. I see little kids racing down the small, dirt hill to pick a pumpkin. Behind them, their parents slowly walk down.

There's one little girl that stands out to me and my sisters. She jumps over pumpkins and screams with delight. I see her coming our way. My nerves tighten and my heart beats faster. She tells her parents to help her pick me and my sisters up.

We are set down on the dry dirt while the parents pay. The little girl looks over at us once in a while and smiles really big, so big you can see some of her teeth are missing.

When her parents are done paying, they pick us up firmly. I look back and see Mr. Smith and Mrs. Smith winking at me.

It is so hard for me to think that I'm actually with a family, ready to be loved. And the best part is that I've got Plumpalicious and Plumpilina with me. I smile and a tear falls down my face.

I look out the car window. The countryside views are incredible. I see green trees on the faraway mountains and yellow weeds behind the iron fence. I can also feel the slight breeze of the wind beside me.

Right then, I think about the birds flying above. They probably feel the breeze too. I am a bird right now. I am in paradise.

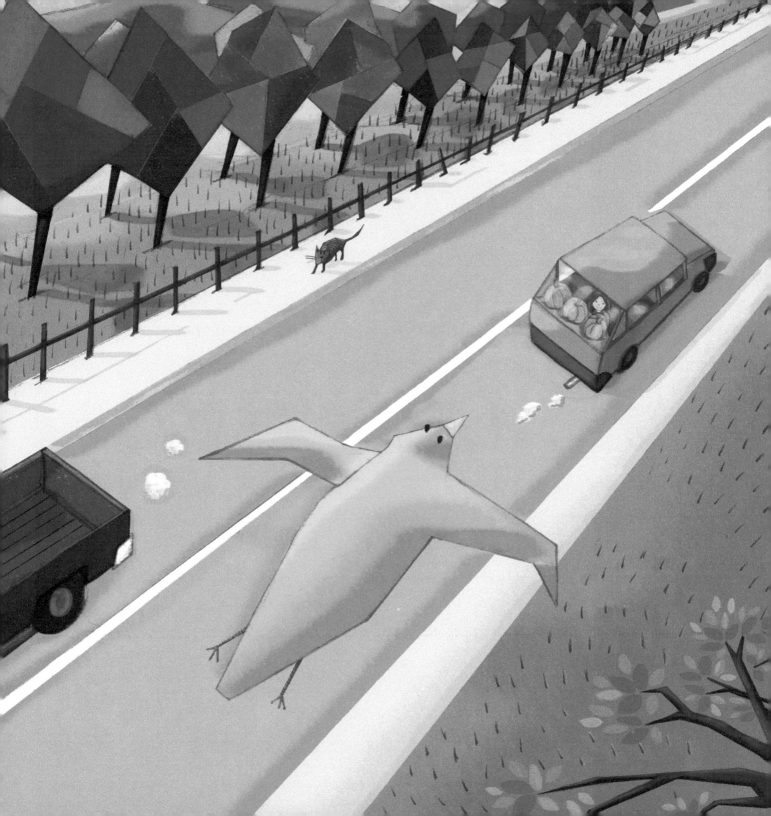

The ride seems long, but I enjoy the cuteness of the little girl next to me. She keeps talking to us and laughing all along. I laugh too, even though I can hardly understand what she is saying. Her liveliness interests me. I wish I was like her.

As we pull up onto the driveway, I see three pumpkins just like us on the lawn of another family's house. I can see that the pumpkins have scary grins, odd noses, and crazy eyes carved into them. I can also see tiny lights inside them, which makes them look like the sun.

The parents take us inside and set us on their table. On the table are various types of tools. The little girl and her father sit down together. The father grabs a tool and starts carving my stem. As he does this, I get so excited. I'm going to get a silly face like the pumpkins on the lawn! Being with a family is even more fun than I imagined it to be.

He circles around my long, emerald stem and picks up another tool. This tool looks like a spoon. He begins to gently scrape the seeds and sets them in a bowl. He continues this with my sisters.

Then, with a different tool, he begins to carve eyes in me. The eyes are round and have frightening eyebrows. Plumpalicious has a stubby nose with a wart on top. I can tell she doesn't like it from the disgusted look on her face. And last but not least, Plumpilina has swollen lips the size of a baby squash.

I guess I'm not the only weirdo in the family now.

Next, the girl opens a box full of candles. One by one the girl places a candle at the bottom of our pumpkin bodies and giggles. I turn my head around and see the mother setting our seeds on a plate to dry them in the sunshine on the windowsill. I am excited. This is the most fun I've ever had in my whole entire life!

The mother, father, and little girl grab us and set us outside next to the other three pumpkins on the lawn. The two adults go back inside the cozy, warm house. But the little girl stays for a moment, watching the six of us. Then she grins and skips back indoors as I lie down with the biggest smile on my face. I glow as the night begins to fall.

The End

CPSIA information can be obtained
at www.ICGtesting.com
Printed in the USA
BVHW020445240919
559231BV00002B/10/P